Dear Parents and Educators,

W9-BVM-404

Welcome to Penguin Young Readers! As parents and educators, you know that each child develops at his or her own pace—in terms of speech, critical thinking, and, of course, reading. Penguin Young Readers recognizes this fact. As a result, each Penguin Young Readers book is assigned a traditional easy-to-read level (1–4) as well as a Guided Reading Level (A–P). Both of these systems will help you choose the right book for your child. Please refer to the back of each book for specific leveling information. Penguin Young Readers features esteemed authors and illustrators, stories about favorite characters, fascinating nonfiction, and more!

Dear Tooth Fairy

LEVEL **3**

GUIDED READING LEVEL **K**

This book is perfect for a **Transitional Reader** who:
- can read multisyllable and compound words;
- can read words with prefixes and suffixes;
- is able to identify story elements (beginning, middle, end, plot, setting, characters, problem, solution); and
- can understand different points of view.

Here are some **activities** you can do during and after reading this book:
- Problem/Solution: There are two problems in this story. The first one is that Robby has not lost any of his baby teeth. This problem is solved when Robby's tooth falls out. But then he *really* loses his tooth. This is the second problem. Discuss how this problem is solved.
- Creative Writing: Pretend you are Robby and none of your teeth have fallen out. Write a letter to the Tooth Fairy. Tell her how it feels to have all your baby teeth. Describe how you would feel if your tooth fell out. Next, pretend you really lose your tooth, just like Robby. Write a thank-you note to the girl who found your tooth.

Remember, sharing the love of reading with a child is the best gift you can give!

—Bonnie Bader, EdM
 Penguin Young Readers program

*Penguin Young Readers are leveled by independent reviewers applying the standards developed by Irene Fountas and Gay Su Pinnell in *Matching Books to Readers: Using Leveled Books in Guided Reading*, Heinemann, 1999.

For Rob—who else!—JOC

To my son Jeff and his fantastic boyhood
pumpkin smile!—JA

Penguin Young Readers
Published by the Penguin Group
Penguin Group (USA) Inc., 375 Hudson Street, New York, New York 10014, USA
Penguin Group (Canada), 90 Eglinton Avenue East, Suite 700, Toronto, Ontario M4P 2Y3, Canada
(a division of Pearson Penguin Canada Inc.)
Penguin Books Ltd., 80 Strand, London WC2R 0RL, England
Penguin Group Ireland, 25 St. Stephen's Green, Dublin 2, Ireland (a division of Penguin Books Ltd.)
Penguin Group (Australia), 250 Camberwell Road, Camberwell, Victoria 3124, Australia
(a division of Pearson Australia Group Pty. Ltd.)
Penguin Books India Pvt. Ltd., 11 Community Centre, Panchsheel Park, New Delhi—110 017, India
Penguin Group (NZ), 67 Apollo Drive, Rosedale, Auckland 0632, New Zealand
(a division of Pearson New Zealand Ltd.)
Penguin Books (South Africa) (Pty.) Ltd., 24 Sturdee Avenue,
Rosebank, Johannesburg 2196, South Africa

Penguin Books Ltd., Registered Offices: 80 Strand, London WC2R 0RL, England

Text copyright © 2002 by Jane O'Connor. Illustrations copyright © 2002 by Joy Allen. All rights reserved.
First published in 2002 by Grosset & Dunlap, an imprint of Penguin Group (USA) Inc. Published in 2012
by Penguin Young Readers, an imprint of Penguin Group (USA) Inc., 345 Hudson Street, New York,
New York 10014. Manufactured in China.

Library of Congress Control Number: 2002007509

ISBN 978-0-448-42849-9   10 9 8 7 6 5 4 3 2 1

ALWAYS LEARNING   PEARSON

PENGUIN YOUNG READERS

LEVEL

TRANSITIONAL
READER

3

Dear Tooth Fairy

by Jane O'Connor
illustrated by Joy Allen

Penguin Young Readers
An Imprint of Penguin Group (USA) Inc.

Class Picture Day was
only two weeks away.
Robby was worried.
He was the only kid with
all his baby teeth.
He was not going to
say "cheese" or smile.
No way!

"What if I am stuck with baby teeth my whole life?" Robby asked his mom at dinner.

His mom told him to stop worrying. But she was always telling him that.

Then she said,
"Why don't you write
to the Tooth Fairy?
After all, she's the expert."
So Robby did.

7

Dear Tooth Fairy,

I have not lost
any baby teeth.
I do not have a
loose tooth.
Can you hurry things up?
        Sincerely yours,
            Robby

The next morning,
Robby found
a letter under his pillow!

Dear Robby,
Please do not worry!
All kids lose their teeth.
Some teeth just take longer
to loosen up.
I repeat. Do Not Worry!

Yours Truly,
the Tooth Fairy

P.S. I can't hurry things up.
It is against the rules.

Too bad the Tooth Fairy could not
help, Robby thought.
Still, it was nice of her to write.
And maybe *he* could hurry things up.

So Robby started wiggling his teeth.

He wiggled his top teeth.

He wiggled his bottom teeth.

"Robby, is something the matter
with your mouth?" his teacher asked
during math.
Robby turned red and said no.
"Then please stop making those faces,"
his teacher said.

Robby had to stop wiggling, anyway.

His tongue was too tired.

And had all that wiggling helped?

No!

His teeth were stuck in as tight as ever.

At lunch,

Robby's friend Steve

stuck two straws

in his holes.

Then Steve sucked up

his milk.

Everybody laughed.

Robby tried not to be jealous.

"Even Jenna has lost a tooth,"
Robby said to his mom at dinner.
"And she is the youngest kid
in our class.
I'm a freak!"

The next morning,

there was another letter

from the Tooth Fairy.

Dear Robby,
I was in the neighborhood
and dropped by.
I wanted to tell you again.
Do not worry.
You will get a loose tooth.
It WILL happen.
        Yours truly,
        the Tooth Fairy

The Tooth Fairy really was so nice.

Robby tried not to think

about teeth.

He really did.

But it was hard.

And then one day,

a bottom tooth moved.

It was the one right in front.

It had a chip in it

from when he was little

and fell off his bike.

Robby was so happy.

He had to share the good news.

That night, he wrote the Tooth Fairy.

Dear Tooth Fairy,

You were right.

I have a loose tooth.
I can't wait to leave it
for you.
I just hope it comes out
before Picture Day.

Yours truly,
Robby

22

The next morning, there was a letter.

Dear Robby,
Hooray for you!
The first tooth a kid loses
is always the best.
I will be waiting for yours!
     Your friend,
      the Tooth Fairy

Every day, Robby's tooth

got looser and looser.

It felt weird but great.

He got a stuffy nose.

Now each time he sneezed,

the tooth wobbled back and forth.

"It's going to fall out any minute,"

Robby told his mom.

His mom said that was great.

But she was not really listening.

She was busy filling up their cart.

Up and down the rows they went.

At the pet food row,

his little sister pointed at his mouth.

"Look! Robby has a hole."

Robby stuck his tongue by his tooth.

His sister was right!

There was a hole.

It tasted salty.

His tooth *had* come out.

But where was it?

"I lost my tooth!" Robby shouted.

"Great, Honey!" his mom said.

"No! No! You don't understand.
I *really* lost my tooth," Robby said.

He was on his hands and knees now.

Where was the tooth?

It had been in his mouth
a few minutes ago.
He remembered wiggling it
over by the meat cases.

"Did you swallow it?"

his mom asked.

Robby shook his head.

"I think maybe I sneezed it out.

It has to be here somewhere."

So they started looking

by the fruits

and frozen foods

and the milk case.

Just his luck,

the floor had black and

white speckles.

"My brother's tooth is lost,"

his little sister shouted.

So other people started looking, too,

even the manager.

But after an hour, still no tooth.

At dinner, his mom said,
"I am sure the Tooth Fairy
will leave a dollar, anyway."
Robby's mom had made spaghetti,
his favorite.
But Robby was not hungry.

"That's not the point, Mom.
The Tooth Fairy has been so nice.
I really want to leave it for her,"
he said.
His mom hugged him.
"She will understand."

Before bed,
Robby wrote a letter
to the Tooth Fairy
about how bad he felt.

The Tooth Fairy wrote back.

She said that it was okay.

She would wait for his next tooth.

She also left a dollar.

But Robby was not happy.

Then at school,

Robby had an idea.

He made a poster.

His friend Steve was

good at drawing.

So he helped.

Robby showed the poster

to his teacher.

She made 10 copies for him.

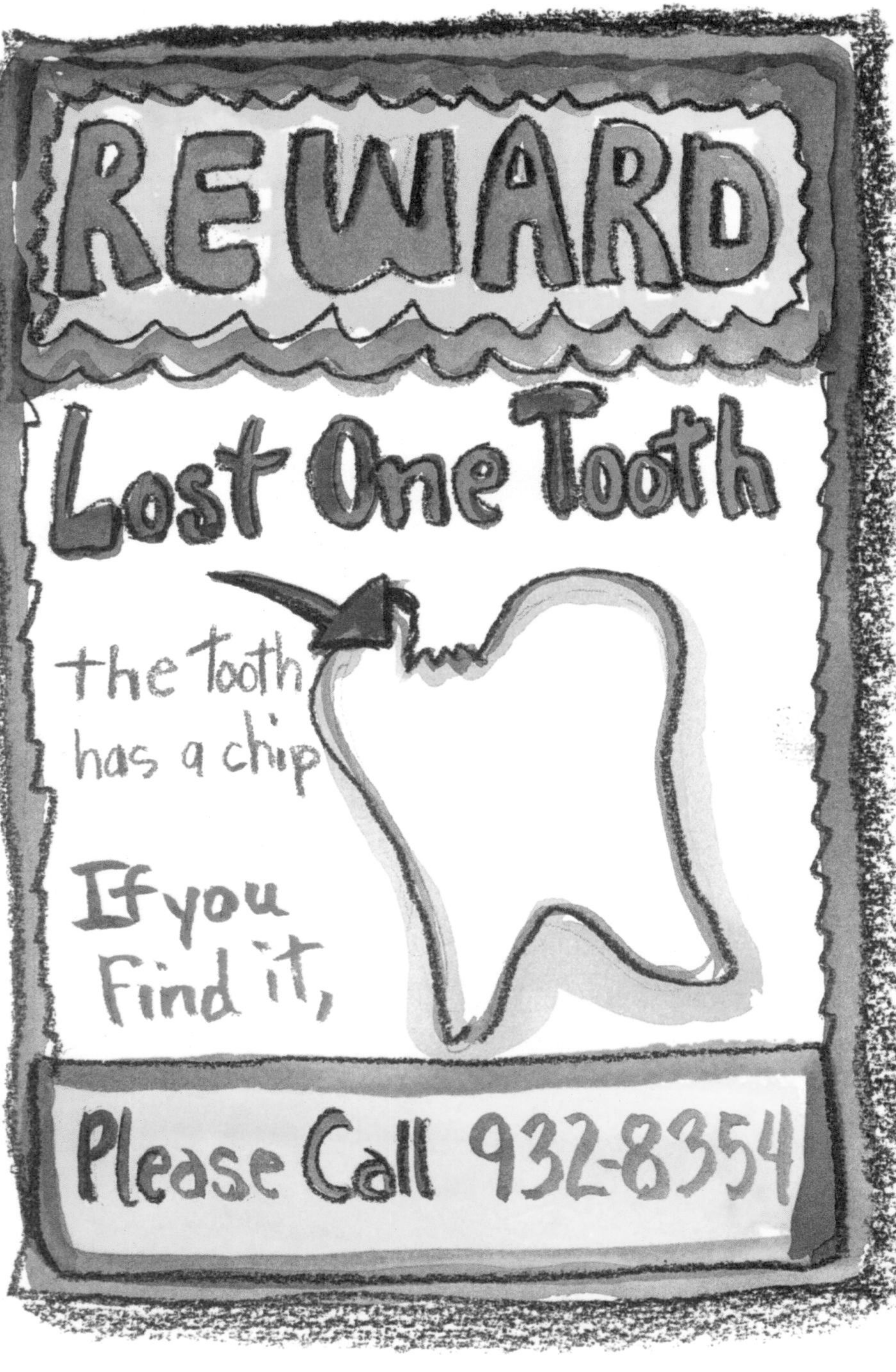

REWARD

Lost One Tooth

the tooth has a chip

If you Find it,

Please Call 932-8354

After school,

Robby biked to the Fast Mart.

He put up all the posters.

Then Robby biked home.

There was no call
that night or the next.
But on the third night,
the doorbell rang.

It was a kid
and her father.
In a plastic bag
was his tooth!

She said,

"We were at the Fast Mart today.

Guess where your tooth was?

On the floor, right by the toothpaste!"

Robby and the girl laughed.

She was missing a tooth, too.

Then he gave the girl the reward—

his dollar from the Tooth Fairy.

That night, he left the tooth
with the chip in it
under his pillow.
He wrote a long letter
about how he found his tooth.
The next morning, the tooth
and the letter were gone.
In their place was a new letter.

Dear Robby,

Wow! You found your tooth!
Thank you sooo much
for leaving it.
I'll always know your tooth
because of the chip.

Yours truly,
the Tooth Fairy

P.S. I left an extra dollar
since you had to pay a reward.

Two days later,
it was Class Picture Day.
Everybody lined up.
"Cheese!" Robby shouted
with all the other kids.
And he smiled a great big smile.
It was a perfect day!